S0-DZH-459

WIDE WORLD

PEOPLE *of the* DESERTS

David Lambert

RAINTREE STECK-VAUGHN PUBLISHERS
A Steck-Vaughn Company
Austin, Texas

WIDE WORLD

PEOPLE *of the* **DESERTS**
PEOPLE *of the* **GRASSLANDS**
PEOPLE *of the* **ISLANDS**
PEOPLE *of the* **MOUNTAINS**
PEOPLE *of the* **POLAR REGIONS**
PEOPLE *of the* **RAIN FORESTS**

Cover: Rajasthani people in the Thar Desert of western India

Title page: Bedouin girls in Dahab, Egypt

This page and Contents page: Huge sand dunes stretching across the horizon in the Namib Desert, Namibia

Published by Raintree Steck-Vaughn Publishers, an imprint of Steck-Vaughn Company

Library of Congress Cataloging-in-Publication Data
Lambert, David.
People of the deserts / David Lambert.
p. cm.—(Wide world)
Includes bibliographical references and index.
Summary: Describes the geography and ecology of desert regions and the history of human activity in some of the major deserts around the world.
ISBN 0-8172-5063-8
1. Desert people—Juvenile literature.
2. Desert ecology—Juvenile literature.
[1. Deserts. 2. Human geography.]
I. Title. II. Series.
GN390.L65 1998
577.54—dc21 98-10915

Printed in Italy. Bound in the United States.
1 2 3 4 5 6 7 8 9 0 03 02 01 00 99

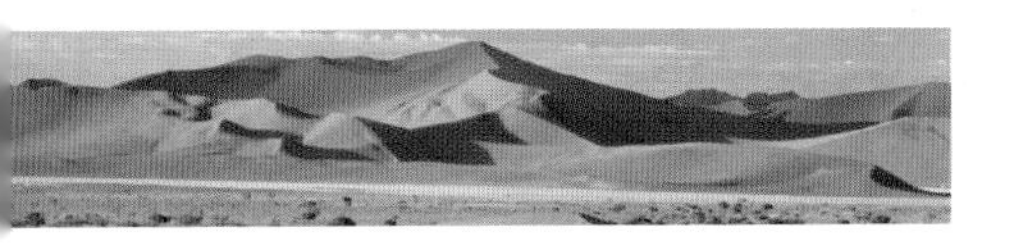

Contents

Desert People	**4**
Dry Lands	**6**
History of Desert People	**10**
Daily Life	**16**
Houses and Settlements	**20**
Work in the Deserts	**26**
Transportation and Communications	**32**
Leisure and Tourism	**36**
The Future	**42**
Glossary	**46**
Further Information	**47**
Index	**48**

Desert People

The World's Largest Deserts

The Sahara Desert	3.5 million sq. mi. 8.4 million sq. km
Australian deserts	598,500 sq. mi. 1.55 million sq. km
Arabian deserts	502,000 sq. mi. 1.3 million sq. km
The Gobi Desert	401,400 sq. mi. 1.04 million sq. km

What do a Tuareg camel driver in Mali, a copper miner in Chile, and a farmer in northwest China have in common? They all live in the harsh, dry environments that are the world's deserts.

Deserts are some of the driest places on Earth. Little rain falls and hardly anything grows. Parts of Chile's Atacama Desert are thought to have had no rain for 100 years. Deserts also include the world's hottest places. In the summer you could fry an egg on the ground in Death Valley, California. The temperature in most deserts drops at night, and some deserts are bitterly cold. You could freeze to death in Mongolia's Gobi Desert during the winter.

▲ A Navajo Indian rancher with a herd of goats in Monument Valley

◀ A young Egyptian boy perches high on a camel's back in the Sahara Desert.

People in deserts

People who get lost crossing deserts can die of thirst, heat, hunger, or frostbite. In the early 1990s, eleven people died when their truck broke down in Australia's Great Sandy Desert. Hundreds of travelers have vanished over the years in Asian and African deserts.

But there are places in deserts where the ground is moistened by water from wells, springs, or rivers. In these places, called oases, plants grow and farms and towns flourish. Most desert people live in oases.

Ancient Aborigines

Over 30,000 years ago, Australia's original inhabitants, called Aborigines, painted pictures in the caves of the Australian deserts. Some of the paintings show the animals they used to hunt. Other paintings tell stories of how the world was made. Aborigines believe that their ancestors came from beneath the earth. When they first came up to the surface, they walked and sang. Every time they sang, they created a new plant or animal. The Aborigines call this period the "Dreamtime."

▼ Rajasthani women winnow wheat in an oasis village on the edge of the Thar Desert of India and Pakistan.

Dry Lands

A desert is an area that has fewer than 10 in. (250 mm) of rain a year, or where the heat of the sun causes a great deal of the rainfall to evaporate. Semidesert areas have fewer than 24 in. (600 mm) of rain. Deserts vary in temperature, depending on their height above sea level and their distance from the equator. Deserts and semi-deserts cover 30 percent of all land on earth. Hot deserts are found in the tropics. Cool deserts are mostly deep inland outside the tropics, or on very dry, tropical coasts.

The desert landscape

Most people think of a desert as a sea of sand, but sand covers only about a quarter of the world's deserts. Most desert terrain consists of bare rock or stones. It is the climate that shapes the desert landscape.

▼ This map shows the world's major deserts.

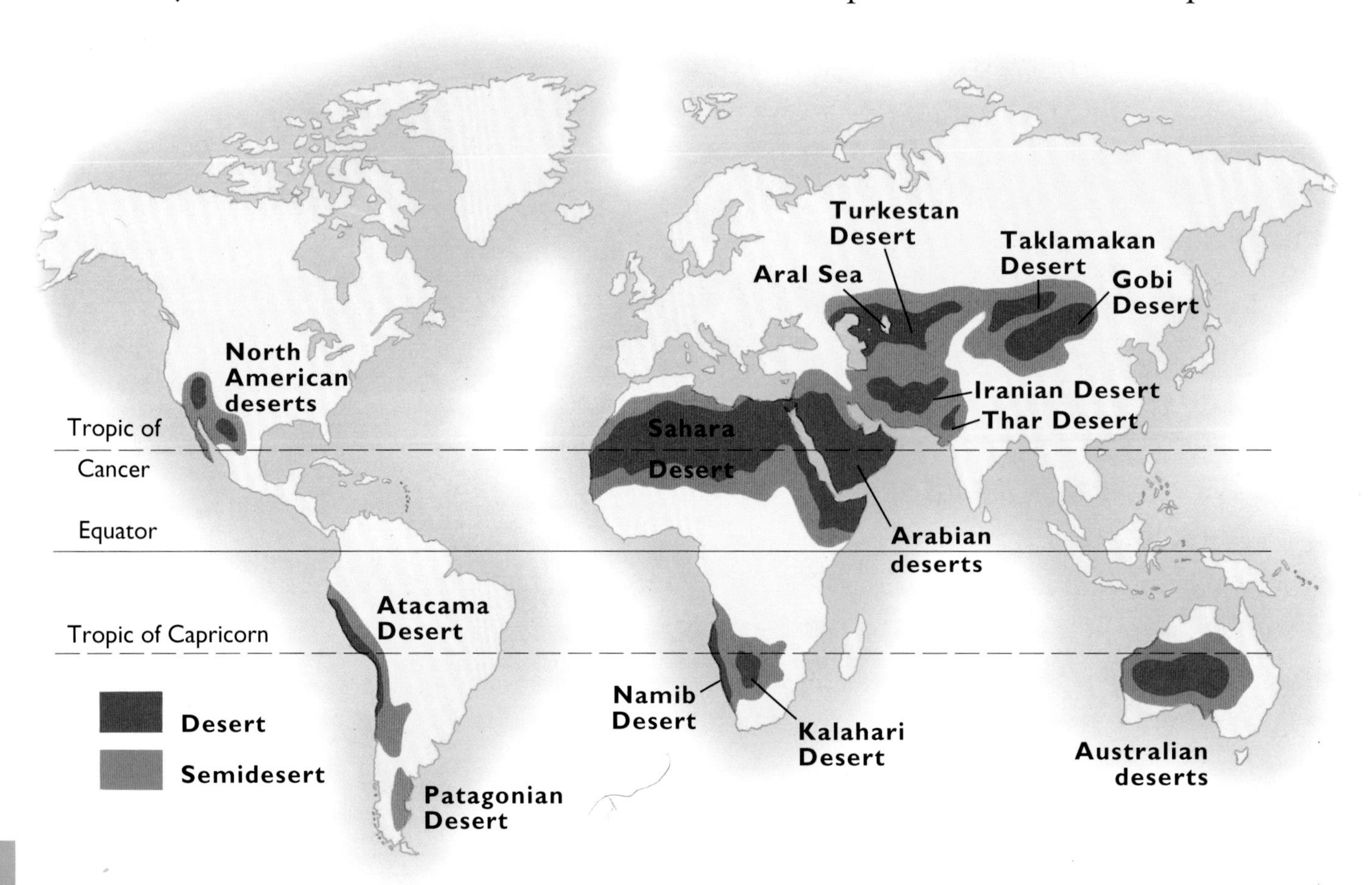

▲ A typical desert landscape in the Namib Desert of southwest Africa, where massive dunes border the sparse vegetation of a desert plain.

In a hot desert, rock heats up and expands by day. But in the cool nights, the rock shrinks. This constant expanding and shrinking weakens the rock until pieces break off.

As desert winds blow dust and sand around, sand grains are thrown against the rocks and stones, wearing them down to a smooth surface. Sometimes, sandstorms and dust storms sweep across deserts. Dust clouds hundreds of feet high can act like a dense, dark fog, and travelers can lose their way.

Where winds blow steadily, they heap the sand and dust into hills called dunes. The world's largest dunes, in the western Sahara Desert in North Africa, are up to 3 mi. (5 km) long and more than 1,300 ft. (400 m) high.

A Dust Storm

Fatima, who lives on the edge of the Western Desert in Egypt, describes a dust storm. "A strong, hot wind called the **khamsin** *blows a great cloud of dust toward you. It grows taller the nearer it comes. Soon its top towers high over your head. Then the cloud swallows you up like a kind of choking reddish-brown fog."*

Water in the desert

Despite being such dry areas, deserts are shaped by water as well as by wind. The little rain that falls often comes in sudden storms. Sudden, heavy rain in deserts can create fast-flowing rivers. These gradually wear away the surface of stones and rock, creating landforms such as wadis (valleys worn in the desert rock). In the Arizona Desert, the Colorado River has carved out the Grand Canyon, the world's largest gorge, over millions of years.

Mirages

In deserts, the intense heat of the sun can play tricks on travelers. Sometimes, people seem to see a shimmering lake where there is only dry sand. The "lake" is really the sky reflected off a layer of hot air close to the ground. Illusions like this are called mirages. Local people are used to mirages, but unwary travelers may stray off the path, believing that they can see water that is not really there.

The town of Dongola on the edge of the Sahara is one of the world's driest places. But during heavy rainstorms in 1988, walls of water washed away buildings after the Nile River burst its banks. More than a million homes in the area were destroyed.

▼ The Grand Canyon is a deep valley nearly 280 mi. (450 km) long, 10 mi. (16 km) across, and more than a mile (1.5 km) deep.

The desert environment

Deserts are some of the most hostile environments in the world. But plants, animals, and humans have all adapted to survive in their harsh conditions.

Desert plants and animals provide a source of food for people who live as nomadic hunter-gatherers. They move from place to place in search of food. The San (who are also known as Bushmen) live in the Kalahari Desert in southwest Africa. While the men hunt animals, the women search for birds' eggs and edible grubs. They dig in the ground for plant roots and bulbs that hold water. Aborigines have done the same in the deserts of Australia for thousands of years.

Wild desert animals, such as antelope in Africa and kangaroos and wallabies in Australia, can be hunted for their meat. But animals such as goats, sheep, camels, or cattle are mostly kept in herds and used for their milk, meat, and hides. Like the hunter-gatherers, herders live a nomadic life and have to keep on the move, looking for fresh grazing for their animals.

A San woman digs for ▶ edible roots and bulbs in Botswana's Kalahari Desert.

History of Desert People

Deserts have been home to people in the Americas, Africa, and Australia since at least the Stone Age, which started about 2 million years ago. They gradually learned how to hunt and gather food and how to find water and shelter.

▼ Anasazi Indians built these cliff dwellings in what is now Colorado, between 800 and 1,000 years ago. Similar dwellings are still occupied by the Hopi people, who are descendants of the Anasazi.

Native Americans

In North America, small groups of Native Americans roamed dry lands west of the Rocky Mountains. They ate what was available, including grasshoppers, rats, snakes, and edible roots. In the California deserts, Native Americans made arrows for hunting by glueing arrowheads to shafts with the sticky gum of creosote bushes. They cooked and ate buds of the spiky yucca trees, and they knew that where bunch grass and mesquite bushes grew they would find water underground.

Farming in the Americas

By 2500 B.C., Peruvian Indians were growing crops beside rivers crossing the coastal desert of Peru. A thousand years ago, the Anasazi living in what is now Colorado dug ditches to take rainwater to fields of beans and corn. They gave up only when the climate changed and their lands became too dry.

▲ This Dreamtime painting shows two characters called the Lightning Brothers. It was drawn by the Wardaman Aborigines of Australia 1,000 to 2,000 years ago.

The Arunta of Australia

For about 30,000 years, the Australian deserts were home to Arunta Aborigines living in small, nomadic family groups. They dug for water in dry riverbeds and drank from dishes made of tree bark. In times of severe drought, the Aborigines would shake the dew off leaves in the morning and even suck water from the stomachs of desert frogs.

Arunta hunters used hooked sticks called spearthrowers to help them throw their spears, which they used to kill emus and wallabies. The Arunta also dug up and ate juicy grubs and honey ants full of sweet-tasting honeydew.

Ancient Art

Long ago, artists painted pictures on rocks in Algeria's Tassili Mountains, deep inside the Sahara Desert. It is not known exactly when the paintings were made but, at that time the Sahara must have had much more rain than today. We know that there were rivers and grassland, and the pictures tell us that herders grazed cattle where now there are only bare rocks and sand.

▲ For thousands of years, Egyptian farmers have used this device, called a *shaduf*, to raise river water to water their crops.

Early farmers and irrigation

Six thousand years ago, Egyptian people living along the Nile River in the Sahara began to change their way of life. Instead of living as hunter-gatherers, they slowly learned to raise livestock and grow crops such as wheat and vegetables. They used the water from the river to irrigate the land. Each year, the river overflowed, leaving silt on the dry land of the riverbank. Crops grew quickly in this damp, rich soil. Egyptians later created more farmland by digging canals and ditches, which carried water to the desert's edge.

Middle Eastern farmers and herders

Canals and ditches were used to supply water to other dry lands of the Middle East. Five thousand years ago, Sumerian farms, villages, and towns flourished on the edge of the Syrian Desert in what is now Iraq. Later, farms and cities also thrived in the Indus River Valley, west of the Thar Desert, now part of Pakistan. Some of the world's first shepherds and goatherds grazed flocks on poor pastures at the edges of Middle Eastern deserts.

Over 2,000 years ago in the Negev Desert in Israel, the people built large terraces (steps) in the desert to prevent rainwater from flowing away, carrying crops and soil with it. They dug channels to carry rainwater into underground caves, where it was stored.

Travel and trade

In the fourteenth and fifteenth centuries, the Tuareg controlled the desert trade in the central and western Sahara. They supplied most of the camels used by Arabian merchants crossing the desert. Processions of hundreds of camels, called camel trains or caravans, trudged north across the Sahara. They traveled to cities such as Tripoli, in present-day Libya, carrying valuable gold, ivory, ostrich feathers, and even slaves to be traded. They brought back salt, brass, cloth, and sugar to be sold at markets in southern cities like Timbuktu, in present-day Mali. Camel trains also brought expensive perfumes from Arabia to Egypt.

Bactrian (two-humped) camels traveled along a trade route known as the Silk Road, carrying silks and carpets from China through the Central Asian deserts to Mediterranean countries. Cities sprang up at oases along the Silk Road, selling food to the travelers.

▼ The ancestors of this Bedouin man first started herding camels, goats, and sheep in Saudi Arabia in the seventh century B.C. The Tuareg of the Sahara became nomadic herders at about the same time.

An engraving showing Burke, Wills, and Gray, who died crossing the deserts of central Australia in 1861.

The spread of Europeans

By the 1800s, Europeans and their descendants in the Americas were exploring deserts previously known only to the local hunter-gatherers or herders.

In the 1820s, René Caillié of France crossed the Sahara Desert. In the 1840s, the British explorer Charles Sturt traveled across the deserts of central Australia, and white travelers first saw California's Death Valley. In the 1870s, Nikolai Przewalski, a Russian, crossed Mongolia's Gobi Desert, and the British traveler Charles Doughty journeyed deep inside Arabia.

Unused to deserts, these Western explorers faced great hardships and dangers. Early travelers called the trek across California's High Desert "the journey of death." In 1861, Robert Burke, John King, William Wills, and Charles Gray became the first four people on record to cross Australia from south to north. Unfortunately, all but John King died of starvation on the return journey.

Danger in the Desert

In the 1940s, Wilfred Thesiger crossed the Empty Quarter in southeast Arabia, the world's largest sand desert. Thesiger wrote: "The sun was scorching hot and I felt empty, sick, and dizzy. As I struggled up the slope, knee-deep in shifting sand, my heart thumped wildly and my thirst grew worse. I found it difficult to swallow; even my ears felt blocked, and yet I knew that it would be many intolerable hours before I could drink."

Westerners and desert development

After the explorers came Western miners, farmers, traders, and fossil hunters. Miners found valuable minerals in desert rocks, and farmers learned they could pump water from huge natural reservoirs in rock deep below the surface of some deserts. Mines, farms, and towns sprang up in some deserts. The mining town of Coober Pedy, in Australia's Great Victoria Desert, developed because of the local supply of precious stones, called opals.

In the 1870s, fossil hunters began to unearth dinosaur bones in the badlands of the western United States. They found it was easier to make fossil discoveries in deserts, which lack plants and soil that can hide fossils. In time, scientists from various countries found the world's biggest sources of dinosaur bones in the deserts and badlands of North and South America, northern Africa, and East Asia. Fossil hunters began working in the Gobi Desert of Mongolia in the 1920s, and by the 1990s had found hundreds of dinosaur skeletons.

▼ The ancient pyramids at Giza, in Egypt's Sahara Desert, were plundered by European museum curators and collectors during the nineteenth century.

Daily Life

Daily life in a desert can vary greatly in different parts of the world. In Arizona, living in the desert city of Phoenix is like living in a city anywhere else in the country. Most people have cars and comfortable houses with refrigerators, washing machines, televisions, and VCRs. They work in stores, offices, factories, schools, or hospitals, and they shop in supermarkets and department stores. People also live comfortably in cities of oil-rich desert lands in the Middle East, although many of their citizens are poor.

Even some small, remote desert settlements enjoy modern conveniences. In Australia's Great Sandy Desert, Aborigines live in tiny groups of government houses supplied with solar-powered freezers.

▼ A Mongol family taking time out for a break of curds and butter in the Gobi Desert. The nomadic people of the Gobi Desert usually travel in family groups.

Disease in the Sahara

Mohammed Yosef lives in Beni Khalid, a Sahara village. He says: "Some of our villagers suffer diseases caused by insects or worms that live in hot places like ours. Flies spread germs that can make people blind from a sickness called trachoma. Mosquitoes and sandflies can give you dangerous fevers. And if you wade or wash in a river or pond, tiny worms in the water could make you very ill with a disease called bilharzia."

Clothing

Because of the extreme conditions in the desert, people often wear special clothes. Many Arab men wear long, flowing robes. Bedouin men wear baggy pants, a shirt under a hooded cloak called a *burnous,* and a headdress like a turban with a heavy veil at the back. In the Sahara Desert, Tuareg men wear turbans and veils that show only their eyes, and loose-fitting blue cotton robes. These clothes help protect the wearers from dust and keep them cool during the scorching hot days. At night, the Tuareg wrap their robes tightly around their bodies to keep themselves warm. In the deserts of Mongolia, which can be extremely cold, people wear many layers of clothing with thick pants and boots made of animal hide and fur.

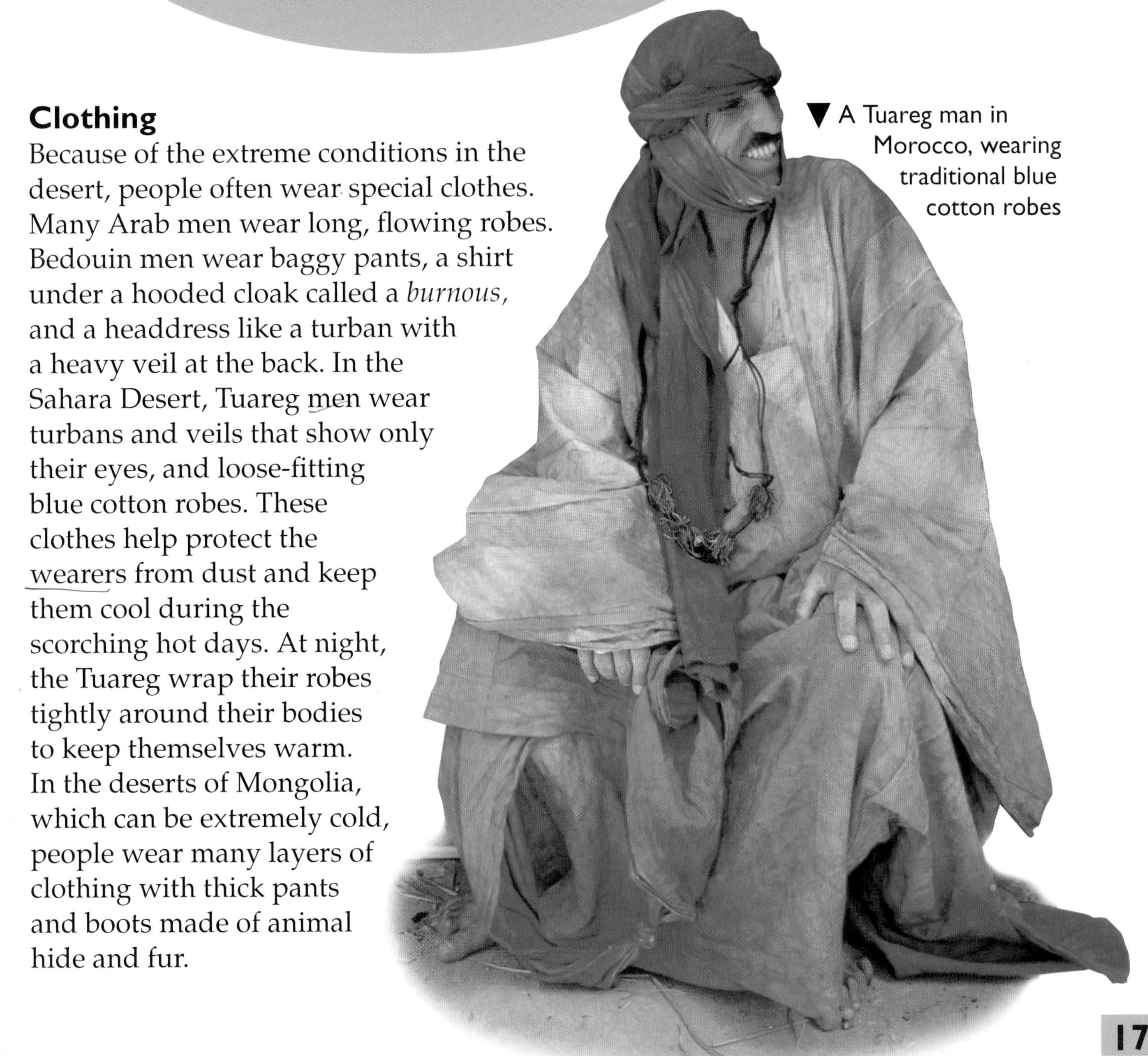

▼ A Tuareg man in Morocco, wearing traditional blue cotton robes

Fuel and water

Daily life can be very hard for people in the Sahara Desert and its remote oases, especially for women, who do most of the domestic chores. There are no machines or even water faucets to make their housework easy. In places like Yatenga province in Burkina Faso, on the southern edge of the Sahara, some women have to spend hours every day just carrying buckets or cans of water from wells. They walk miles to gather firewood or dried dung to use as fuel to cook the family's meals.

A Desert Oven

After a successful hunting trip, the Aborigines of the Australian deserts traditionally dig a hole in the ground, using a boomerang as a spade. They line the bottom of the hole with stones and leaves and put the meat on top. When they seal the hole, the intense heat in the ground cooks the meat in a few hours.

Food

Desert farmers often grow most of their own food, and herders rely heavily on the milk and meat from their animals, especially when they are far from the nearest town or village. Camels, goats, and sheep provide plenty of milk, and the women turn most of it into yogurt, butter, or cheese. The foods most Bedouin women prepare come from the family's herds or from crops grown in oases. Bedouin women mix flour and water into pancakes of dough and bake these over a fire to make bread. They also cook mutton or camel-meat stews.

Scalding hot coffee or tea are the favorite drinks of various Saharan peoples. Bedouin hospitality is famous, and families offer coffee to all passing strangers.

◀ Women hauling water from a well in Mali, on the edge of the Sahara Desert

▼ People in the desert often buy and sell food and goods at open-air markets like this one in Luxor, Egypt.

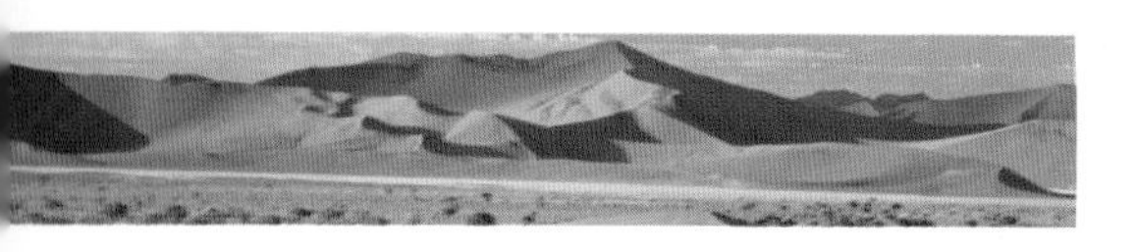

Houses and Settlements

Traditional housing

Before concrete, glass, and other modern building materials were available, desert peoples made their houses from local materials. In parts of some deserts, people still live in traditional dwellings. For example, at the Tinerhir Oasis in Morocco, people use the leaves of locally grown date palm trees to make the roofs of their houses. They put wooden shutters on the windows, which they close during sandstorms.

Nomadic peoples, such as the Tuareg, Bedouin, and Berber, need lightweight, portable homes and usually live in tents made of canvas, animal hide, or woven wool, supported by a wooden frame. The wandering Mongols of the Gobi Desert live in a type of tent called a *ger*, made of animal skins or canvas.

▼ This Berber's broad, low tent provides shelter from the heat and strong winds of the Sahara.

◀ Caves make cool homes in the Saharan oasis town of Matmata, Tunisia.

Mud bricks

In desert oases from the southwest United States to China, mud bricks are the easiest building blocks because they are made from natural materials. Mud bricks are made by mixing sandy earth with water and straw and pressing the mixture into a brick-shaped mold. When the soft brick has dried, it is left out in the sun to be baked hard. The walls of adobe (mud) houses are often covered with a kind of smooth plaster called stucco.

Keeping Cool

In Iran, builders create cool homes in an unusual way. They use mud bricks to build houses with tall "chimneys" called wind towers. The wind blows down these towers and through the rooms below. The moving air keeps people cool.

An adobe house can be cooler than a wooden or stone building. Hot deserts are the only places where mud-brick houses last well. Frost makes them crumble, and rain tends to wash them away. Many Arabs, Iranians, Pakistanis, Indians, and Chinese still live in mud-brick houses today, as do the Pueblo Indians of Arizona and New Mexico.

▼ The walls of adobe houses, like this desert house in Rajasthan, India, are often painted white to reflect the heat and keep the interior cool.

▲ The city of Marrakech in Morocco provides work for thousands of people in its factories, offices, stores, and markets.

Desert cities

Efficient irrigation systems have allowed many new desert settlements to grow in places where, previously, water was so scarce that farming and even daily life would not have been possible. Many desert towns and cities have grown up during the twentieth century, as people have moved to them to look for work or a more comfortable lifestyle.

Migration

In the United States, a steady flow of people move from colder parts of the country to work or retire in the warm southwest. Here, cities like Phoenix, Arizona, have housing developments and apartment buildings specially built for retired people. Jewish people from all over the world have moved into new settlements built on desert and semidesert land in Israel. Since World War II (1939–1945), people in Central Asia have swarmed into oasis towns and cities to work in factories set up by China's Communist government.

Nomadic herders and poor farmers in North Africa have been leaving dry lands to find work and housing in oasis towns and cities like Cairo, beside the Nile River in Egypt. Cairo has grown into one of the largest cities on Earth.

Living Underground

In the mining town of Coober Pedy in Australia's Great Victoria Desert, people have built their homes underground to escape the hot days and cold nights. There is even an underground hotel.

In Saudi Arabia, most Bedouin have stopped roaming the deserts. They have found work and more modern living conditions in cities. The government encourages this migration, which makes it easier to collect taxes and also provides more workers for the growing oil industry. Saudi Arabia's capital, Riyadh, was once just a small oasis town. Today, thanks to the oil industry, Riyadh is a bustling city of more than 2 million people. Besides local people such as the Bedouin, there are many migrants from abroad. For example, many construction workers and domestic servants in Riyadh have moved there from Pakistan.

▼ Apartment buildings have sprung up to house the growing population in Syria's second-largest city, Aleppo.

Modern settlements

As people flock to live in desert cities, the settlements grow. Modern concrete apartments, office buildings, and shopping malls spring up around the old parts of cities, which usually have traditional low, flat-roofed houses crammed between narrow lanes.

Driving through wealthy desert cities such as Phoenix, Arizona, you would see rows of houses surrounded by green, watered lawns. Only the solar panels on the roofs might seem unusual. The hot sun heats water flowing through pipes in these panels, which supplies a free hot-water supply to each household. Air-conditioning systems keep the temperature pleasantly cool in houses, stores, restaurants, movie theaters, and cars.

Traditional Style

Some of the most modern Arab buildings include traditional features. In Oman, modern concrete apartments with delicately arched windows are built around a garden swimming pool, rather like the rooms of an old Arab palace. The huge terminal of the Saudi airport at Jedda has a fiberglass roof resting on poles nearly 160 ft. (50 m) high to make it look like a row of giant Bedouin tents.

▼ All Saharan towns once looked much like this old city area of El-Qasr, Egypt.

Water in cities

Water is piped to desert cities from wetter areas, pumped up from underground wells, or channeled from rivers. Many city yards have swimming pools and grass lawns. Even golf courses are watered by sprinklers.

In the city of Dhahran in Saudi Arabia, thousands of Saudi and U.S. oil workers and their families live in neat rows of bungalows, each with a lawn watered by underground wells. Machines pump the water from deep underground, where rainwater has collected over thousands of years.

A process called desalinization is sometimes used to remove the salt from seawater. For example, in Riyadh, this process helps to provide water for the city's growing population. But desalinization requires expensive technology, so only wealthy countries can afford to use it.

▲ Water from the Colorado River is used to water flowerbeds and fields in the city of Phoenix, Arizona.

Work in the Deserts

Desertification

Nomadic herders like the Fulani and the Tuareg face new problems as crop farmers take over more of the land on the southern edge of the Sahara Desert. This forces the herders to graze their animals in a smaller space. Over time, the land loses its trees, plants, and soil and gradually becomes part of the desert. This process, by which the deserts gradually expand, is called desertification.

In deserts or their oases, most people live by hunting, raising crops or livestock, trading, or mining. Traditional lifestyles are changing as people find new ways to make a living. For example, most of Africa's San people and Australia's Aborigines no longer live as hunter-gatherers. They work mainly on ranches or farms on the edges of deserts instead.

A Bedouin girl ▶ cradles a young goat. Petra Beidha is twelve years old and lives with her herding family in Jordan.

Herders and shepherds

For hundreds of years, camels have been used for transportation. They are also kept for their hide, milk, and meat, as well as for their hair, which is used for weaving. Even their dung can be dried and used as fuel. Today, there are still people from groups such as the Bedouin of the Arabian Peninsula, the Tuareg of the Sahara, and the Mongols of the Gobi Desert, who depend on camels for food, transportation and as a source of income. Even rich Bedouin living in cities often keep camels out in the desert. Today, however, they drive them to fresh grazing land in trucks or vans.

▲ Camel herders trading at the Pushkar camel fair, an important event in the Indian state of Rajasthan

Hot deserts where camels thrive are too dry for cattle, sheep, or goats. However, in North Africa and southwest Asia, herders tend townspeople's flocks of sheep and goats in pastures where there is water for the animals to drink.

In the semidesert fringes of the Sahara, herders like the Fulani keep as many animals as they can. This means that they are unlikely to lose a whole herd if there is a drought. A big herd also shows that a herder is important in the community.

Farming

In North African oases, traditional farming methods are still in use. Where water lies near the surface, farmers grow dates by digging holes in the sand and planting groves of date palm trees in the moist soil. Some groves cover a very wide area and have more than 200,000 trees. Each day, farmers may have to shovel away windblown sand that can bury the date palms.

Water from a well irrigates ▶ these vegetables, grown in an oasis of Kordofan, a region in the central part of Sudan.

Farmers in oases like Matmata in Tunisia till the ground with hoes or plows pulled by camels. The leaves of date palm trees provide other crops with shade from the hot sun. At the Tinerhir Oasis in Morocco, farmers use this shade to grow millet and sweet potato. At Matmata, beans, onions, and watermelons are grown in the shade, and the farmers also raise fruit trees, including apricots, figs, peaches, and pomegranates. Barley and wheat sprout in the open ground, where fences made from palm leaves keep drifting sand away from the crops.

▼ Cucumber plants flourish in the desert of Oman, thanks to irrigation ditches that bring water to moisten their roots.

Irrigation

To irrigate crops, desert farmers pour water into ditches that run across the fields. Much of the water comes from wells dug in dry riverbeds.

At the Algerian oasis of Ghardaia, camels, donkeys, or mechanical pumps work day and night, operating machinery to raise water from wells. In Libya and in Texas, motor-powered pumps suck up water from thousands of wells. In the southwestern United States and in Egypt, Syria, and Pakistan, rivers have been dammed, creating lakes that supply water to desert farms. Huge mechanical sprinklers move slowly across the fields, spraying them with water.

At Advat, in Israel's Negev Desert, water is dripped through holes in plastic pipes above the crops so that each plant gets just the right amount of precious water. Irrigation like this even allows the farmers of Advat to grow orchards of peaches, cherries, and almonds.

Locusts

In North Africa and southwest Asia, huge swarms of insects called locusts can attack crops, stripping a field bare in a matter of minutes. Ada Solomon, who lives in Israel's Negev Desert, says: "Millions of locusts once landed on our fields and ate our crops. There were so many they made the sky dark. We had to use the car's wipers to brush them off our windshield as we drove along."

Where water can be supplied to fields in huge amounts, farmers can grow and sell large crops, such as cotton, corn, sugarcane, and potatoes. In Libya, there are circles of irrigated land in the Sahara so huge that they can be seen from space.

Irrigation makes farming possible in many desert areas, but too much water can make the ground waterlogged. As water evaporates in the hot sunshine, it also brings to the surface salt from underground. Most crops will not grow in waterlogged or salty soil, and in Iraq, for example, nearly half the land is now too salty to grow crops.

▼ A boy with a bundle of sugarcane near Kom Ombo, in Egypt

▲ Many desert people make a living by trading their goods at markets, such as this one in the Algerian town of Ghardaia.

Business and trade

In oasis towns, many people spend their working day making or buying and selling goods. For example, in North African towns, men make carpets and brassware by hand. In western China, men work largely in factories or as traders. On Sundays, peasants stream into the Chinese oasis city of Turfan, driving flocks or donkey carts to the bazaar. Traders buy and sell donkeys, goats, horses, and camels, and people sell cotton and silk goods, grapes, melons, spices, and poultry from market stands. Some even pedal bicycle-powered machines to turn sheep's milk into ice cream.

Oil industry

In the deserts of Saudi Arabia and Kuwait, many thousands of people work in the oil industry, finding the oil, bringing it to the surface, building pipelines to carry oil from wells to oil tankers, transporting it to factories or ports, and working at refineries, where the oil is turned into gasoline and other useful products such as plastics and paints.

▼ Engineers working at the Burgan oil field in Kuwait

More oil is produced near the Persian Gulf than anywhere else in the world, and Saudi Arabia's Ghawar oil field is the largest on earth. Money earned by selling their oil abroad has made previously poor Arab countries like Kuwait and Saudi Arabia amazingly rich, although the wealth is not evenly spread among the people.

Mining

Mining is big business and a major source of employment for desert people and workers from abroad. Parts of some deserts are now home to more miners than farmers or herders. Miners extract minerals such as iron ore, coal, diamonds, copper, and bauxite.

At Mount Newland in Western Australia, workers drive machines that scoop up iron ore from the ground in gigantic mechanical shovels. Mount Newland is a mountain of iron ore, which is gradually shrinking as it is mined. The iron ore is transported by railroad about 300 mi. (500 km) to the coast, where it is used to make steel at Port Kembla.

▼ Workers operating heavy machinery at a coal mine in New Mexico

Transportation and Communications

In the twentieth century, the introduction of roads, railroads, air travel, and vehicles that can cope with rough landscape has made it easier to travel in the desert. However, desert travel today can still be dangerous and difficult for travelers.

Animals

Probably the most important animal for the people of the deserts is the camel. There are two types of camel—the one-humped Arabian camel of Arabia and Africa, and the two-humped Bactrian camel of Central Asia. Both are still widely used today. Camels are well adapted to desert conditions and can survive for up to ten days without water, making them ideal pack animals. In South America, alpacas and llamas, relatives of the camel, are used to carry small loads in the Atacama Desert of Chile and Peru. Horses are sometimes kept near desert edges where there is enough grazing and water, and they can be a symbol of importance for rich sheikhs. However, they are not widely used, since they are not adapted to the hot, dry desert climate.

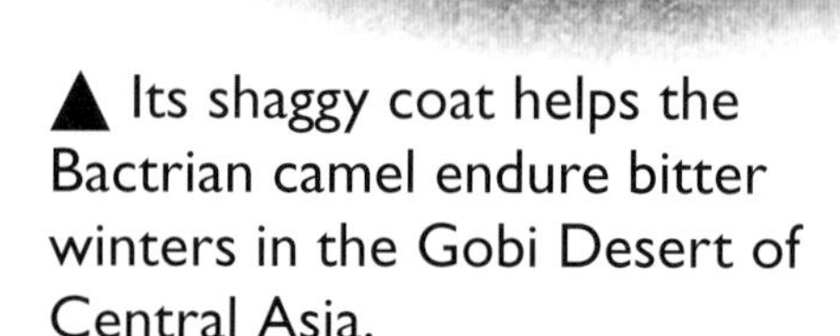

▲ Its shaggy coat helps the Bactrian camel endure bitter winters in the Gobi Desert of Central Asia.

▼ A llama train carries its light load across the Atacama Desert in Peru.

Road travel

Today, most desert transportation is mechanized. Wealthy farmers and traders drive four-wheel-drive vehicles with big tires for gripping soft sand. In poorer countries, people travel in crowded buses, carrying produce or livestock to sell at the nearest market.

Good paved roads cross deserts in the United States and oil-rich countries beside the Persian Gulf, although shifting sands sometimes bury part of a road. Most other desert routes are just tracks left in gravel or sand by the tires of vehicles. Following tracks across a hot, sandy desert is dangerous. You can die if your vehicle breaks down or gets stuck in the sand or if you get lost or run out of drinking water.

Truck drivers in Sudan cross the Sahara Desert in convoys, so that if a truck breaks down, they can help each other. They take plenty of water and set off at night when it is cooler and the tracks they follow show up in the headlights. They carry mats and spades, so that if a truck gets stuck, its driver can shovel away the sand and put the mats under the wheels to give them grip.

▼ Truck drivers stop for a rest as their convoy makes the difficult journey across the desert of Sudan.

▲ A four-wheel-drive vehicle crosses a rough, rocky region of the Sahara Desert.

Driving in the desert

Many drivers take four-wheel-drive vehicles racing and rallying over some deserts. In one popular North American event, drivers speed down Mexico's long, semi-desert peninsula of Baja California. On weekends in the United States, crowds of southern Californians drive off-road vehicles into the desert east of Los Angeles.

Attempts to break the world's land-speed record have taken place in Nevada's Black Rock Desert and in the desert of Jordan. Long, flat, smooth stretches of sand give powerful cars room to build up tremendous speed, and there are no trees or buildings to hit if they go out of control.

Railroads

A few major railroads cross deserts. The world's longest straight stretch of railroad track runs 330 mi. (530 km) across Australia's treeless Nullarbor Plain. The longest train in the world is a 1.8-mi. (3-km) long train that crosses the Sahara, carrying iron ore from Mauretanian mines. In Central Asia, thousands of Chinese workers shifted mountains of sand to build a railroad through the desert to oasis cities. They still work to keep the track free from sand. Desert trains are often crowded with people, animals, and goods. In the Sudan, people who cannot afford to buy train tickets sit on the roofs of railroad cars.

Damaging the Desert

Modern vehicles allow people to travel in the world's deserts, but they can also do serious damage. Driving over the sandy ground can break up the thin surface crust so that sand is blown away, exposing the roots of plants, which then die. The tires of vehicles have so badly damaged parts of the desert in California that the government has closed it to traffic.

▲ Small airplanes are used to deliver mail to the scattered inhabitants of the vast, empty regions of northern Australia.

Air travel

Invisible air routes now pass over big deserts, and most long-distance travelers choose this way to go. Flying has become the fastest, easiest, and safest way of crossing a desert. Each year, hundreds of thousands of Muslim pilgrims from around the world fly to Jedda in the desert country of Saudi Arabia to visit a shrine called the Kaaba, in the city of Mecca.

Keeping in touch

Being able to send and receive news is very important to people crossing a lonely desert or living in an oasis cut off from the outside world. By the 1970s, drivers who broke down on desert roads in Saudi Arabia could call for help, using a roadside solar-powered radiophone. People living in Alice Springs in the Australian Desert can now use telephones, fax machines, or e-mail to contact people thousands of miles away.

▲ Wherever he goes, his car telephone keeps this Bedouin businessman in touch.

Engineers have set up huge dish antennas in deserts to track satellites circling the earth. Now, communications satellites beam down television programs to remote desert settlements such as Alice Springs.

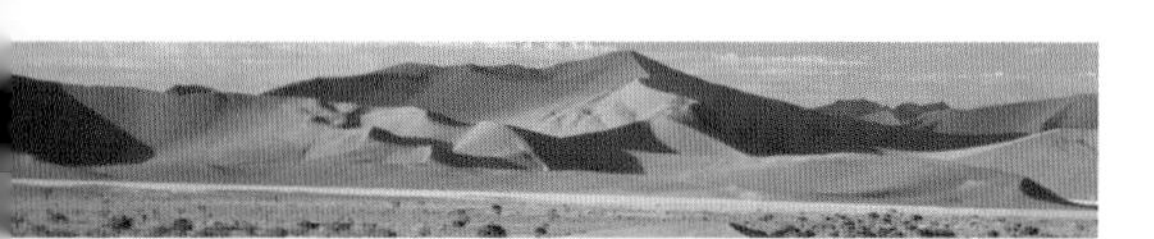

Leisure and Tourism

People spend their spare time in deserts in many different ways. In desert cities, leisure facilities are similar to those in any other cities of the world, from restaurants and bars to theaters and sports centers. The use of irrigation means that wealthier people can enjoy luxuries such as swimming pools, gardens, and golf courses. Electrical goods are becoming smaller and easier to carry, and most desert people who can afford them own cassette and CD-players, radios, and television sets.

▼ This Native American woman is weaving a rug to sell to tourists in the desert landscape of Monument Valley.

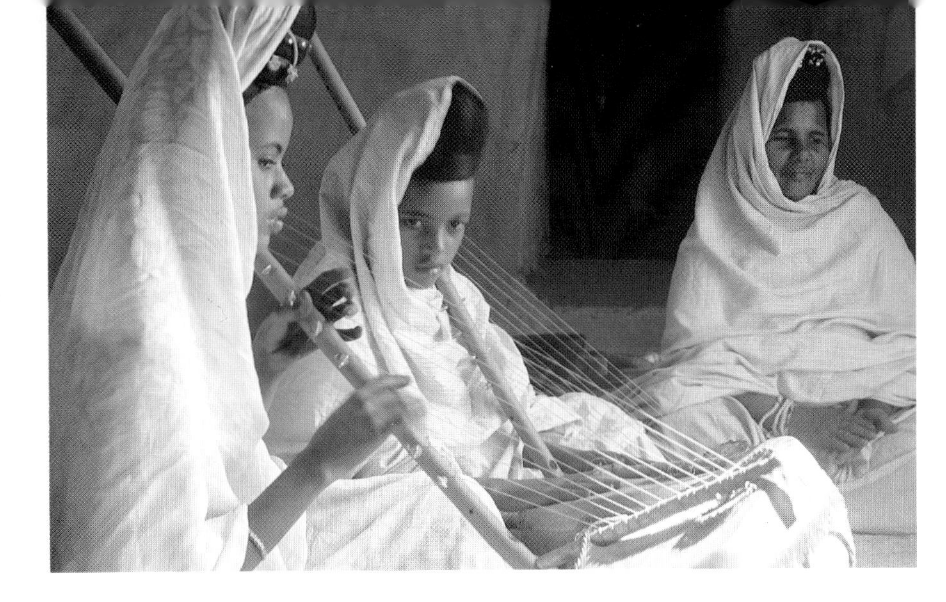

Nomadic people and those living in smaller settlements often do more traditional leisure activities. These include hunting, sports and games, dancing, and playing traditional musical instruments, such as the Bedouin fiddle or the Aboriginal didgeridoo.

▲ These Berber girls in North Africa are playing traditional stringed instruments.

Weaving is popular among the nomadic Mongols and the Bedouin, who weave the wool of their sheep, goats, or camels. They make colorful blankets, clothing, cushions, and rugs, which they can either use themselves or sell to tourists. Weaving is a source of income for some Navajo people of the American southwest, along with their traditional silver and turquoise jewelry. Many nomadic Tuaregs also make and sell jewelry. Other traditional desert crafts include pottery, leatherwork, beadwork, carving, and metalwork.

Desert peoples, especially nomads who spend much of their lives traveling, often get together for festivals and celebrations. The Aborignal *corroboree* is a traditional gathering that allows people from separate groups to meet and enjoy music, dancing, and storytelling.

▼ The Aboriginal didgeridoo is a traditional musical instrument, made from a long, wooden pipe.

▲ Children as young as five race camels in the United Arab Emirates.

Races

Camel races have long been popular in the Arabian Peninsula. Early each Friday morning in winter, young riders urge their camels around a racetrack at Ras Al-Khaimah in the United Arab Emirates. Once a year, a much bigger camel race takes place in Saudi Arabia. Thousands of riders and camels head out across desert sands for the 14-mi. (22-km) King's Camel Race. The winner receives prizes that include money, a water-carrying truck, and a gold dagger.

A far stranger race takes place at the Henley-on-Todd Regatta in Alice Springs, Australia. The event takes its name from the boat races held at Henley-on-Thames in England, but the Todd River race takes place in a dry riverbed, and the boats have no bottoms. The contestants in the boats run along, carrying their boats with them.

◀ Barefoot teams run a desert boat race along the dried-up Todd River in Australia.

Desert trips

Visiting deserts can be an exciting adventure, especially for city people. In Morocco and Tunisia, tourists travel out into the Sahara Desert, sometimes driving great distances, taking enough food, fuel, and water to last for days and camping out at night.

Other visitors to deserts come on package tours, attracted by the desert landscape and wildlife. In southwest Africa, tourists come to see the animals that thrive in the Kalahari and Namib deserts. Other desert tourist attractions are strange rock formations, like the tall rock towers of Monument Valley, Arizona. One of Australia's most famous sights is Uluru (which used to be known as Ayers Rock), a huge hump of red rock in the flat desert of central Australia. Uluru is a sacred place for the Aborigine Pitjanjara people.

In the Middle East's deserts, most tourists come to admire ancient monuments preserved by the dry weather. Every year, people from all over the world flock to Egypt to visit the famous ancient pyramids. Many visitors take river trips up the Nile to see ancient Egyptian temples and tombs. These tourists travel in comfort in elegant ships that are floating hotels.

A tourist photographs ▶ the ancient statue of Rameses II, near Luxor in Egypt.

Desert vacations

Vacationers often visit hot deserts to enjoy a warm winter break. The air-conditioned hotels that have sprung up in desert oases can make even scorchingly hot desert weather bearable for visitors.

▲ Tourists in southern Tunisia taking a camel trip into the Sahara Desert

▼ Mountain bikers on the edge of the Western Sahara in Morocco

At the Desert Shade resort in Israel's Negev Desert, visitors stay in big tents like those of the Bedouin and are treated like the Bedouin's guests. They explore the desert on camels or in four-wheel-drive vehicles. Israel is also home to the famous desert seaside resort of Eilat, where people bask in winter sunshine and go scuba diving in the Red Sea.

Retired people probably take more desert vacations than anyone else. In the United States, large numbers of elderly people drive down to Arizona from the cold north to spend warm winter months camping in trailer parks in the desert.

Las Vegas

The city of Las Vegas grew up in a desert valley first discovered by explorers in 1850. Today, Las Vegas is the fastest-growing metropolitan area in the United States. It is home to eleven of the world's twelve largest hotels. In 1997, the world's largest hotel was the MGM Grand Hotel-Casino in Las Vegas.

Palm Springs and Las Vegas are two of the most famous desert resorts in the southwest United States. In the 1930s, Palm Springs in southern California became a favorite spot for Hollywood movie stars to visit. Today, Las Vegas in southeast Nevada is a center for casinos and luxury hotels.

A couple on a hiking trip ▶ set up camp on a desert ridge in Utah.

The Future

In the future as desert towns and cities grow, houses and industries will need more food and water. In richer desert countries, irrigation can be used to turn more areas of desert into farmland. However, by taking underground water, people are rapidly using up the supply, which will one day run out. For example, cities in the southwestern United States are using up the water faster than rain can replace it.

Cities will have to find better ways of producing food, water, and power, which do not exhaust the desert resources. Desalinization is the process of taking the salt out of seawater. It is one way of producing water without using up the underground supply. Solar energy is another way of producing renewable power, and it is also cheaper and cleaner than burning oil or coal.

▼ A desalinization plant in Oman. It takes the salt out of seawater so it can be used by homes and industries.

Spreading the deserts

The world's deserts are spreading as poor desert people try to grow more crops and livestock than the dry land can support. Plants are cut down for firewood and killed by overgrazing, and water supplies dry up. With no plants left to hold it together, the soil blows away in the wind. Once the soil is gone, desertification occurs as land on the edges of deserts slowly becomes part of the desert.

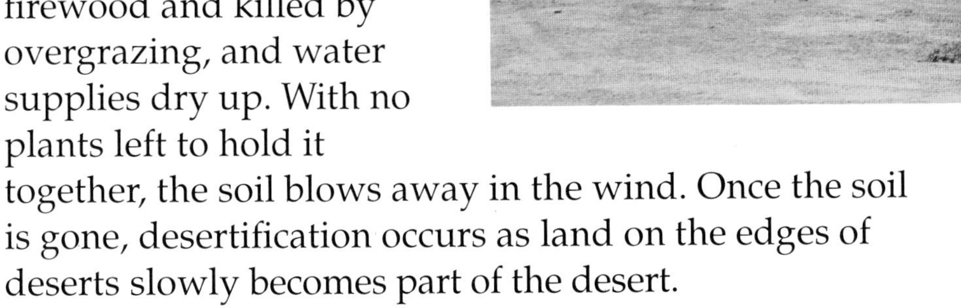

▲ Four-wheel-drive vehicles like these damage the desert environment and hasten the process of desertification.

▼ Huge dunes threaten to swallow up the crops at this Libyan oasis, which relies on irrigation to survive.

▲ Workers in Mauritania in West Africa build brushwood fences to keep the desert sand from blowing away.

Repairing the damage

People can do much to keep the deserts from spreading, and even push them back. In Burkina Faso in West Africa, local people have developed a successful way of stopping their land from turning into desert. They place lines of stones across their lands, so that when the rains come, the stones prevent the soil from being washed away. The people then plant crops on the moist land.

Farmers can make better use of the water they have. In Israel's Negev Desert, water is piped to crops growing inside long plastic tents. As the water evaporates in the heat, it is prevented from escaping and runs back down inside the tents to water the plants again. This allows farmers to use far less water than they would on crops grown in the open air. Farmers can adapt to drought by growing crops that need very little water. Experts also think that many small farms would make better use of desert land than just a few huge ones.

Desert populations are growing. If they are going to survive in the future, people need to use the desert resources carefully and find ways of preserving their environment.